Morris the  Mankiest Monster

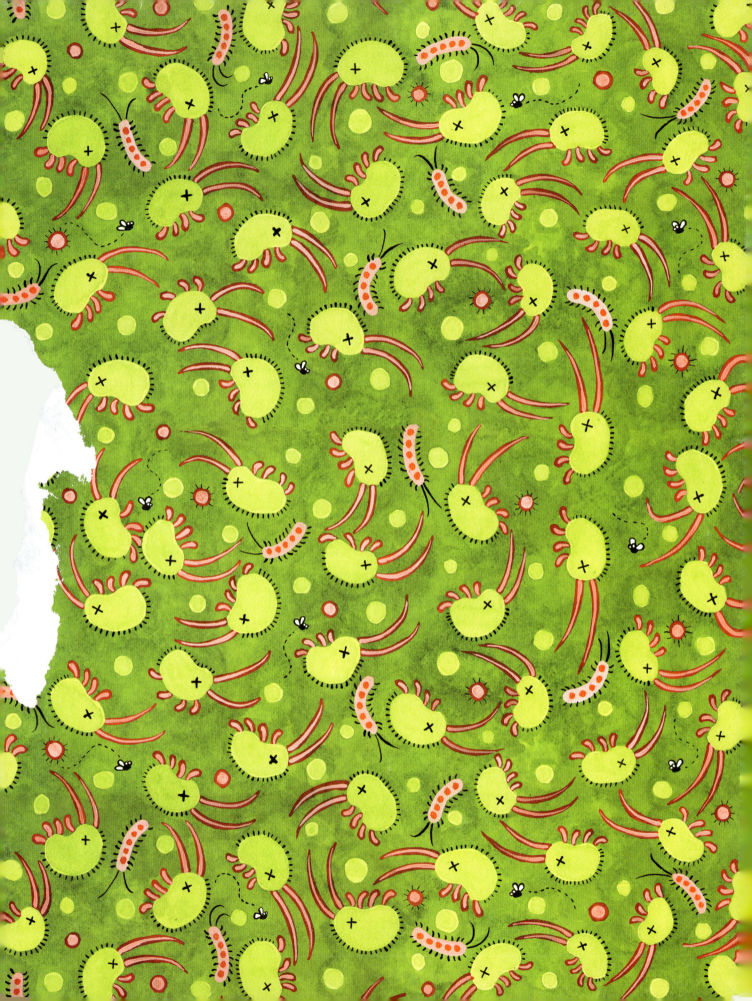

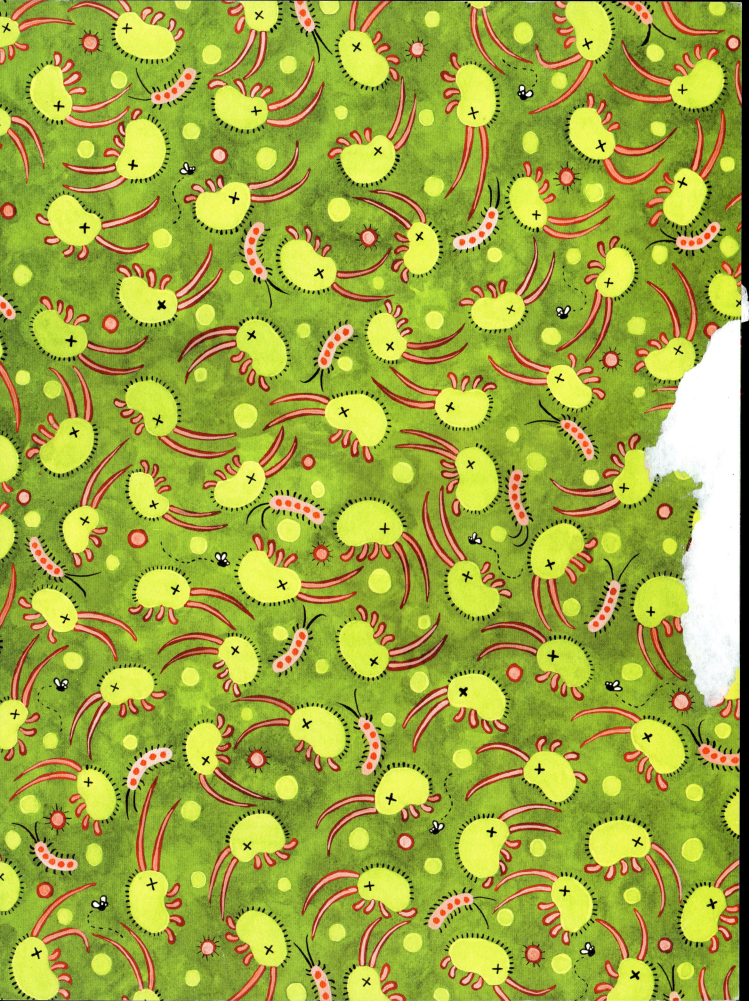

For Jackson - G.A
For Stuart - S.M

MORRIS THE MANKIEST MONSTER
A PICTURE CORGI BOOK 978 0 552 55935 5

First published in Great Britain by David Fickling Books,
a division of Random House Children's Publishers UK
A Random House Group Company

David Fickling Books edition published 2009
Picture Corgi edition published 2010

7 9 10 8 6

Text copyright © Giles Andreae, 2009
Illustrations copyright © Sarah McIntyre, 2009

The right of Giles Andreae and Sarah McIntyre to be identified
as the author and illustrator of this work has been asserted in accordance
with the Copyright, Designs and Patents Act 1988.

Picture Corgi Books are published by Random House Children's Publishers UK,
61-63 Uxbridge Road, London W5 5SA

www.randomhousechildrens.co.uk

Addresses for companies within The Random House Group Limited
can be found at: www.randomhouse.co.uk/offices.htm

THE RANDOM HOUSE GROUP Limited Reg. No. 954009

A CIP catalogue record for this book is available from
the British Library.

Printed in China

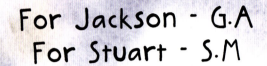

PICTURE CORGI

Morris the Mankiest Monster

Written by
Giles Andreae

Illustrated by
Sarah McIntyre

Morris
the
mankiest
monster . . .

. . . Lives in a house made of **dung**

It only smells **stinky** enough when it's damp So he keeps the walls wet with his **tongue**

He sleeps in a bed of
old compost
Shovelled on
lovely and **thick**

And when he gets up
he goes into the
bathroom

And gives all his
scabs a good pick

His cheeks are encrusted with **pustules**
Which **dribble** like hot melted cheese
Warm yellow wax **oozes** out of his ears
And his eyebrows are riddled with **fleas**

His forehead's all clammy and sticky

His breath reeks of rotten fish paste

And goodness knows what
he collects in the creases
And **great** folds of
fat round his waist

If you look under
his armpits
You're bound to
find loads of
dead bugs
He munches and crunches
them in between meals
And then flosses
his teeth with
fresh slugs

He feeds off the **snotty green bogies**
That lurk up his **big** hairy nose
And sometimes he **nibbles** the poisonous mould
Which he scrapes **off** the ends of his toes

He washes this down with
cold snail slime
Collected from
underneath rocks
But just to make sure that
it's tasty enough
Morris filters it first
through his socks

It's years since he last
changed his t-shirt
It's **crusty** and crawling with ants
His shoes are all **slurpy**
and **squelchy** inside
And potatoes grow
**out of his
pants**

His fingernails
badly need cutting
They're
**terribly
grimy**
and black

He uses them
daily to
scratch
at his warts
And to **squish**
the big boils on *his* back

If Morris starts feeling
too tidy
He always knows just
what to do
He has a long bath in
the SEWAGE canal

And then
Washes
his hair
in the
loo

You may think he's
foul and **disgusting**
But really, in spite of all this
There's nothing
he loves more
than making new friends . . .

... So he's coming to give YOU a KISS!

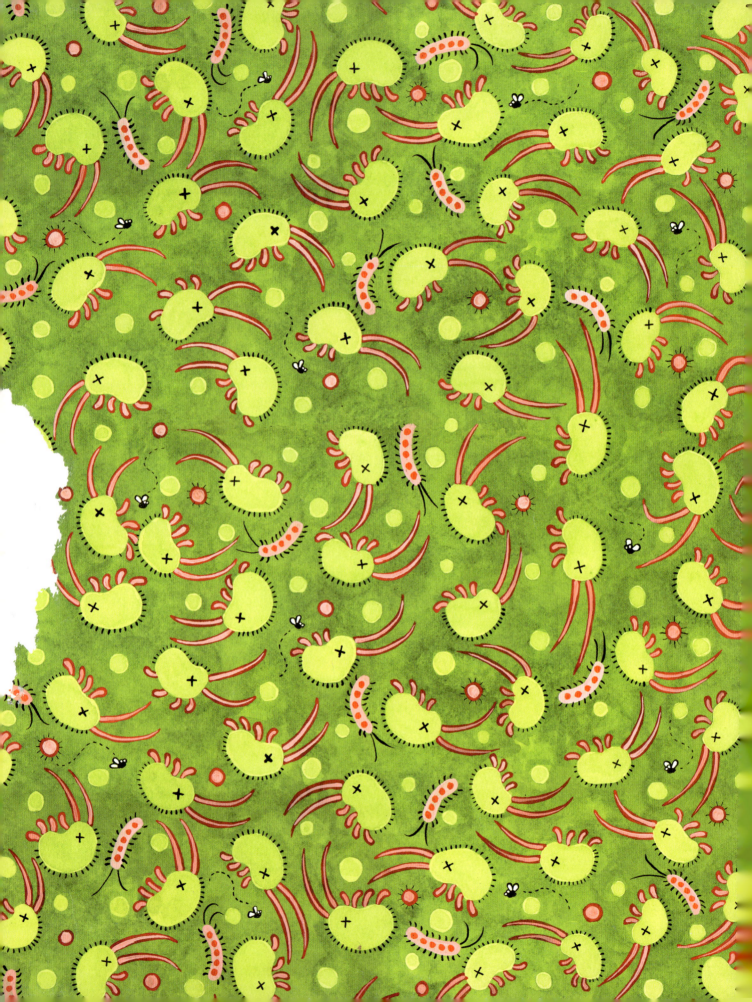

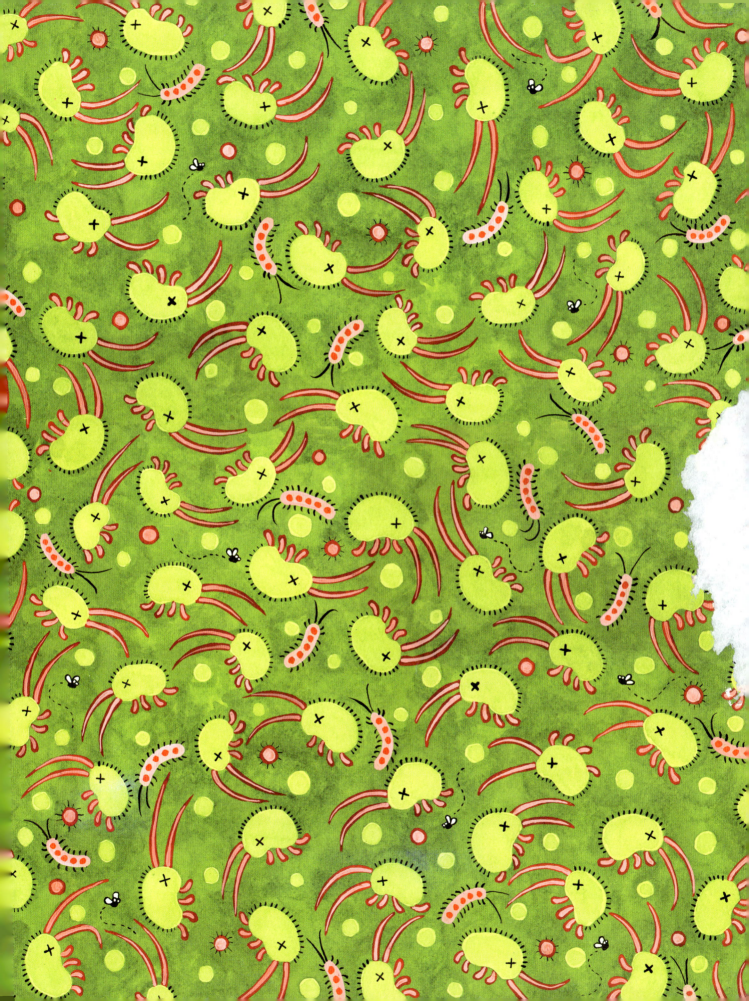

If you liked

Morris the Mankiest Monster,

you'll love . . .

Pants &
More Pants
by Giles Andreae and Nick Sharratt

Shark in the Park! &
Shark in the Dark!
by Nick Sharratt

Grizzly Dad
by Joanna Harrison